A PRECARIOUS PREDICAMENT

ou swim in every direction, looking wildly for a sign of your friends. You have no idea which way is which. But no matter where you swim, you find only whitecaps. Your heart sinks. The *Trilobite* is gone forever.

The storm is starting to let up. Through the thinning rain, you think you see something. You look closer at the shape emerging from the water.

 If you swim toward it, turn to page 28.

 If you swim away from it, turn to page 9.

Only you can decode the 3-D stereogram and make the decision that will lead to your escape—or to your destruction!

BOOKS IN THE SUPER EYE ADVENTURE SERIES:

PREHISTORIC ISLAND

By Jay Leibold

Illustrations by Ray Zone and Chuck Roblin

A Byron Preiss Book

BANTAM BOOKS
NEW YORK • TORONTO • LONDON • SYDNEY • AUCKLAND

007-012

PREHISTORIC ISLAND

A Skylark Book/November 1995

Skylark Books is a registered trademark of Bantam Books, a division of Bantam Doubleday Dell Publishing Group, Inc. Registered in U.S. Patent and Trademark Office and elsewhere.

Super Eye Adventure is a trademark of Byron Preiss Visual Publications, Inc.

Special thanks to Timothy Robinson and Beverly Horowitz.

Cover painting by Phillip K. Zimelman
Cover design by Heidi North
Illustrations by Ray Zone and Chuck Roblin
Typesetting by Maryland Linotype

ISBN 0-553-48323-4

Published simultaneously in the United States and Canada

PRINTED IN THE UNITED STATES OF AMERICA

0 9 8 7 6 5 4 3 2

HOW TO READ A STEREOGRAM

In this book you will enter the fantastic world of 3-D stereograms. Stereograms are based on cutting-edge computer technology that takes advantage of the way the brain sees. Our two eyes each see a different 2-D picture of the world. Our brain takes these two images and merges them into one 3-D image. Random-dot stereograms, like the ones in this book, have two identical patterns hidden on either side of the page. When looked at a certain way, the patterns come together—to make one eye-popping picture!

There are twenty stereograms in this book to help guide you through the weird landscape of Prehistoric Island, past dangerous dinosaurs, man-eating mammals, and treacherous volcanoes. The stereograms will help you decide where to go and what to do next. Only if you can decode them will you be able to make your escape!

How do you read a stereogram? There are two primary ways. One method is to hold the stereogram up close to your face, almost touching your nose. Allow your vision to blur. Then move the page slowly backward, until it is about eight inches from your face. If your vision remains unfocussed, you should be able to see the 3-D image.

The other method is to use two black dots at the top of the stereogram. Hold the page about eight inches from your face and let your vision blur. Now you should see four black dots instead of two. If you gaze long enough, the two middle dots should merge into one. When you move your eyes down the page, the 3-D picture will come into view.

Now you're ready for your first stereogram. Turn this book on its side so that the black-and-white pattern is above this page. The two square black dots should be at the top. Now follow one of the two procedures for decoding stereograms described above. You should see something that you will meet on your journey. Do you see it? If you do, turn the page and begin your adventure!

 Turn to page 1.

"We crossed into the Bermuda Triangle last night!" you hear a voice say.

The Bermuda Triangle? Curious, you look up from the book you are reading. You are on the deck of the *Trilobite*, a scientific research vessel bound for South America. That means you'll be spending the summer with a team of scientific experts doing your favorite thing in the world: digging up prehistoric bones!

You earned your place on the expedition by knowing just about every animal that ever walked, crawled, slithered, or swam on the face of the earth. But just to make sure you can hold your own with important scientists, you've brought along a few dinosaur books.

Two famous paleontologists are standing a few yards away from you and talking now. "The Bermuda Triangle is nothing but a geographic location in the Caribbean Sea bounded by Florida, Bermuda, and Puerto Rico. But the crew is all jumpy. They're terrified of this little patch of water."

"Yes, there's talk of getting lost in some time warp, or a parallel universe."

"Right, that's a good one. Beam me up!" cracks the first scientist. They both chuckle and start to walk on when another voice murmurs from over by the steering house, "It's no joke."

It's Ernesto, one of the deckhands. He catches your eye and says very solemnly, "A lot of people have disappeared in the Triangle. Ships sink, people drown, planes just vanish. *Perdido*—no one hears from them again."

He just stares at you for a moment and you get a sinking feeling in your chest.

Bill, the first mate, suddenly appears. "Ready for your next scuba lesson?" he asks you.

A bonus of your voyage is that Bill has been teaching you to scuba dive. You go astern with him to don your gear. As you pull your mask over your face, you pause a moment before diving in. That's Bermuda Triangle water, you remind yourself. But it's a clear blue day, and Bill splashes in without hesitation. You follow.

You soon forget your doubts. Bill is teaching you how to stay underwater for longer and longer periods of time. You dive deep into the tropical waters and follow a school of silvery fish, always being careful to keep Bill in sight. It hardly seems like fifteen minutes before Bill jerks his thumb upward and you begin your ascent.

Ten feet or so before you reach the surface you can tell something is wrong. The blue skies are gray and filled with clouds. You break the surface with a splash and find yourself smack in the middle of a tropical gale that must have come out of nowhere.

Thunder booms in your ears and lightning cracks the sky. The ocean swell has become huge. The *Trilobite* appears and disappears from view as you rise and fall on the giant waves. Your heart is racing.

"Bill," you yell. You can hardly hear your own voice. Then you see him on deck with Ernesto. They are calling to you. "Grab this!" Bill calls, throwing a life preserver at you.

You manage to get your hands on it. Ernesto tries to pull you in, but the storm is so fierce and ferocious that it won't let him. The line snaps.

Desperately you swim for the boat on your own. But it's no use. The slanting rain and howling wind carry the *Trilobite* farther and farther away. It has no power to maneuver in the storm.

Then a tremendous bolt of lightning strikes. Electricity crackles all around you in a ring of fire. It rises above you and explodes in a ball of white light.

You pass out—only for a moment, you think. Luckily the life preserver keeps you afloat. But when you come to, there's no sign of the *Trilobite*.

You swim in every direction, looking wildly for a sign of your friends. You have no idea which way is which. But no matter where you swim, you find only whitecaps. Your heart sinks. The *Trilobite* is gone forever.

Or is it? The storm is starting to let up. Through the thinning rain, you think you see something. Could it be your ship? You look more closely at the shape emerging from the water.

 If you swim toward it, turn to page 28.

 If you swim away from it, turn to page 9.

You turn around and swim toward where you last saw the *Trilobite*. At least, you *think* you're going the right way. When you shook off that giant shrimp, you got yourself a little shaken up, too.

You swim round and round, scanning the horizon for some glimpse of your friends. They wouldn't just sail off without you, would they? But all the while you can't shake the creeping feeling that you're not in the same waters anymore. After all, there were no extinct jumbo shrimp in the seas you were sailing on the *Trilobite*.

Your muscles are beginning to ache and your hopes are sinking. You decide that if there's land nearby, you should swim for it before you meet up with that giant shrimp again. With your remaining strength, you turn around and head for the shape you see on the horizon.

 Turn to page 14.

You back away from the stump. "Hey, Ralph," you call, "can we go a different way? These burned-out trees are creepy."

Ralph shrugs and leads you out of the burned area. You wander through the hills and forests of the island. After a few days it's obvious that you're doing nothing but going around in circles. Ralph has no idea how to find the Time Blatt, and neither do you.

One night you have a vivid dream. In it, a man in fancy clothes with a cape and boots and a plumed hat appears. He holds a sword and points with it to a tree stump where the words "Look here" are carved.

You wake up and tell Ralph, "Look here! That's what was carved on that burnt stump. I think we passed up an important clue. Let's go back and check."

You return to the lightning-struck area.

Turn to page 42.

"Nice mastodon," you say in a soothing voice, holding up a leafy branch to the huge, snorting, obviously hungry creature that has stopped right in front of you. "Nice boy. Here, have a bite to eat."

Mastodons, you know from your studies, are vegetarians. You figure you have nothing to fear from this one as long as you can keep it happy with some jungle salad.

But then it opens its mouth. There's definitely something different about this mastodon—it's got unusually sharp teeth for a plant-eater. In fact, they're not the teeth of a plant-eater at all. . . .

You turn to escape. But before you can take two steps, the mastodon's got you forked on a tusk like a piece of meat. You make a delicious meal—low in fat and full of protein.

The End

"*Y*ow!*" you exclaim in disbelief when you see the monster shrimp rising from the deep to look for food.

You recognize it instantly from the picture in one of your books—*Anomalocaris*, a creature that thrived on prehistoric fish in the Paleozoic era. The Paleozoic began 570 million years ago!

But there's no time to ponder about what it's doing here. One of its huge claws snaps just short of your leg and you swim madly to escape. Fear propels you ahead. Its bulbous eyes revolve like periscopes on stalks, searching for you. This is the ugliest bit of seafood you've ever seen. It gives new meaning to the term *jumbo shrimp*.

You keep changing direction as you swim and the hungry monster seems to lose track of you. Finally it returns to the deep from whence it came. The storm clouds, which came upon you so suddenly, are disappearing, too. It's as if the whole thing were a dream—except that you're still treading water in the middle of the Caribbean Sea, alone except for a gargantuan crustacean that became extinct 225 million years ago.

You know from studying the charts last night that there is no land within miles. And yet—what is that shadow looming on the horizon? Can you make it out? Should you swim for it? Or should you turn and keep searching for the *Trilobite*?

 If you keep swimming straight ahead, turn to page 14.

 If you swim the other way, turn to page 6.

"Yes!" you cry, picking out the shape of one volcano rising above the rest. But how will you get there?

You look down into the gorge of seething waters. "There's got to be a way to do it," you say to Ralph.

For a moment, a shadow passes overhead. You hear a great *whoosh*, then feel air flow across your face. Something has landed behind you. Something that doesn't belong at the beginning of time. You wonder: *Has it come to help us? Or is it there for some other reason?* It seems to be beckoning you.

 If you climb aboard what you see, turn to page 79.

 If you don't think that's such a great idea, turn to page 16.

No matter what the charts say, that's land you see on the horizon. This is the Bermuda Triangle, after all. What was it those scientists were joking about—time warps, parallel universes?

You swim for the land with nice even strokes. It seems to take forever. Finally the surf deposits you on a sandy beach. There you pass out from exhaustion.

When you open your eyes again, the sun is shining down upon you. Palm fronds wave above in a gentle breeze. You can almost imagine you're on a tropical vacation. But your predicament slowly comes back to you: This is no vacation. You're stranded on a beach that isn't even supposed to exist!

You sit up with a start and brush the sand out of your eyes. A hulking shape is silhouetted against the sun. Is it animal or vegetable? Friend or foe?

 Turn to page 29.

You tend to agree with Ralph. Jumping onto a giant quetzalcoatlus, the largest flying creature in the history of the world, might be a really stupid idea.

"There's got to be a better way to get to the volcano," you say as the two of you slowly back away from the enormous winged reptile. Ralph grunts in agreement. The quetzalcoatlus just ignores you.

You keep walking along the edge of the precipice, looking for a way to get across the seething cauldron of fire and water between you and the volcano. Finally you discover a break in the precipice through which you can go down to the water. A series of broken rocks appears to form a low bridge across the river.

"This must be the way," you tell Ralph.

You hop and skip from rock to rock. Chunks of fiery lava rush past you in the churning water. Ash falls from the sky like snow.

Suddenly there is a tremendous boom above you. It shakes the earth—and you—to the core like nothing you've ever felt. You look up. The volcano directly above you is erupting. The sky is red with fire. A giant avalanche of red-hot lava, rocks, boulders, and ash rushes down the mountainside.

"Fire river coming for us!" screams Ralph.

You look wildly for an escape route. But there is nowhere to go. Lava is everywhere. You and Ralph are destined to become one of the world's first rock groups!

The End

Reee. . . *arkh!*

The man-eating mastodon lets out a bellow and comes lumbering after you. You turn and dash up the hill. You duck into the nearest cave just in time to escape a stabbing tusk.

Relieved, you gulp in huge breaths of air. Confused thoughts run through your mind. No mastodon fossil you've ever seen had teeth like that one did. Not only are mastodons supposed to be vegetarians—they're supposed to be extinct, which is what you'll be if you don't figure out what's going on.

"This is a very, very strange island," you say out loud.

"Heh-heh," a low voice says from the back of the cave.

You jump. Then you sit very still and listen. Now you hear heavy breathing. Something is in the cave with you. You peer into the darkness but can't see a thing.

You're about ready to dash back out and take your chances with the mastodon when a whiff of something familiar hits you. Only one creature makes that smell.

"Look, Mr. Caveman, I'm not going to play hide-and-seek with you. You can come out now."

The caveman scrambles forward to squat next to you. You move away a couple of feet and give yourself some breathing space. The fellow gives you a yellow-toothed smile and says, "Island strange." He shakes his hairy head in wonder. "Tuskface eat human. Rrrwwff never see that where he come from."

"What did you say your name was—Ralph?" Ralph nods. You introduce yourself, then continue. "Ralph, where *do* you come from? And do you have any idea where we are now?"

Ralph shrugs. "Where me come from, everyone looks like Rrrwwff. Not like sea monster." He looks at you and snorts.

"Now, time all mixed up," he tells you. "Angry noise, big snakefire in sky bring Rrrwwff here. Must find Time Blatt."

"Time Blatt," you mutter, figuring it's some Neanderthal superstition. You poke your head outside the cave. The coast is clear. You crawl out and take a deep breath of fresh air. Ralph is right behind you, tugging on your elbow and going on about how you must help him find the Time Blatt.

"So, where is this Time Blatt?" you finally ask.

Ralph shrugs. "Don't know."

You sigh with impatience. You just want to get a signal fire built before the *Trilobite* gives up on you and leaves the area. Suddenly you point up and cry, "Hey! Look! A flying saucer!"

While Ralph scans the sky, you run over the hill and down the other side. Ralph seems like a nice enough guy for a caveman, but you're afraid he'll just get in the way.

You notice that someone has dug a deep pit in a hollow on the other side of the hill. You avoid it as you resume your wood gathering, your ears peeled for more mastodon thuds. All you hear are a few crackling noises. You figure they're just forest sounds. Yet you've got the annoying impression that you're being spied upon. "Okay Ralph, enough fun and games," you say. But there's no reply.

You hear another crackle and whirl around. There's something poking through the leaves on a branch in the tree right above you! What is it? Should you drop down and curl into a ball? Or jump into the big pit to your left?

 If you curl up into a ball, turn to page 24.

 If you jump into the pit, turn to page 33.

Slowly you turn and look out over the landscape to the west.

"Well?" Ralph shuffles his feet, obviously impatient. "Which way to go?"

What do you think?

 If you decide to go east, turn to page 66.

 If you decide to go west, turn to page 45.

You drop to the ground and curl up into a ball. You remember hearing that predators won't attack prey in that non-threatening position. And the huge fangs poking through the leaves of the tree above you definitely belong to a predator. A saber-tooth tiger, to be precise!

You don't make a sound, don't make a move. You hear the big cat emerging from its hiding place in the leaves. You feel a soft thump as it drops to the ground. It pads almost soundlessly toward you.

Then you remember something else you read: *Most* predators will leave a curled-up animal alone. Cats are the exception. Nothing draws their curiosity like a motionless, helpless animal curled up like a ball.

You take a peek up at the tiger. Its paw is raised, ready to strike.

With your last breath you remember how your kitten at home likes to toy with a mouse before she eats it. Now you know how the mouse feels.

The End

Ralph points to a nearby mountain. "We go to top. Get view. Find Blatt."

You climb to the top of the mountain with Ralph. An incredible panorama opens up before you. You feel as if the entire history of the earth is laid out at your feet, more glorious than anything you've ever seen. A lump comes to your throat.

Off on the horizon you see smoke rising. "The furnace at the beginning of time," you whisper in awe. "Isn't that where Señor Rodrigo said we would find the Time Blatt?"

"Yes, furnace," Ralph agrees.

Looking more closely, you see that there are two ways to get to the fires of the furnace. One route lies to the east of the mountain, the other to the west. The two very different landscapes are separated by a deep canyon.

"Which way do you think, Ralph?" you ask.

Ralph shrugs and throws it back to you. "Great wizard choose. Rrrwwff can build raft or can walk with big lizards."

You study the landscape to the east intently. Do you

want to go this way? Or do you want to look at the west-
ern landscape?

 **If you decide to go east, turn
to page 66.**

 **If you want to study the west
first, turn to page 22.**

You put your head down and swim as fast as you can toward the large shape coming up out of the water.

"Thank goodness I was lucky enough to find the *Trilobite* in this storm," you say to yourself. "The Bermuda Triangle won't claim me after all."

No, the Bermuda Triangle will not claim you. But the giant man-eating shrimp rising from the deep will. If you thought it was a boat, you must not have gotten a very good look at it in the storm.

You barely have time to wonder what *Anomalocaris*—the scientific name of a gigantic shrimp that became extinct 300 million years ago—is doing in the Caribbean Sea before the monster grabs you in its claws. It doesn't matter now. You are about to become the shrimp's cocktail.

Tartar sauce anyone?

The End

As your eyes adjust to the light around the strange figure above you, you let out a gasp. But before you can get to your feet, the man pulls at the hair on his chest and runs from you screaming.

"Hey, what's so scary about me?" you call after the fleeing figure. After all, *he's* the one with hair all over his body, a club in his hand, animal skins for clothes, a stout jaw and a bulging brow—not to mention his peculiar smell. If you didn't know better, you'd swear he was a Neanderthal caveman from a previous stage of human evolution.

Then you look down at yourself. You're clad in a black wetsuit, with fins on your feet, a diving mask on your head, and an oxygen tank on your back. A caveman might take you for some hideous creature from the sea. But he *wasn't* a caveman—was he?

"Anything's possible, after that shrimp," you mutter to yourself. You shed your mask, tank, and fins and set off into the dense forest that crowds the beach. You want to collect enough wood to start a signal fire on the bluff above one end of the beach—just in case the *Trilobite* is still out there.

Inland from the beach, the landscape is full of ravines and hills dotted with caves, but something seems out of place to your trained eye. The vegetation doesn't seem tropical. The leafy trees here remind you of a more temperate climate.

Collecting the wood is hard work. Soon you take off your wetsuit, too, saving only your waterproof belt pack containing survival supplies.

As you gather the wood, you begin to hear mysterious deep rumblings. What could they be? Distant thunder? Cannon fire? Neither seems likely.

Whatever the rumblings are, they're getting closer. You hurry back toward the beach with an armload of wood. But you don't get far before the earth starts to shake beneath your feet. You turn to look behind you. What do you see?

 If you offer up a leafy branch, turn to page 8.

 If you try to flee to a cave up the hill, turn to page 18.

Let's go back in the direction of the dinosaurs," you say to Ralph.

"Meat!" Ralph says, pointing to the giant twenty-foot sloth standing on its hind legs to eat from the upper branches of a tree.

It's a truly incredible creature, though you can't imagine what it would take to kill it. "We don't want to go that way," you explain to him. "That's a megatherium. It's a mammal from the Pleistocene period, which is very recent. We want to go back in time so we can find the Time Blatt. That means we should go back toward the dinosaurs."

Ralph lets out a disappointed grunt. You climb back out of the gorge on the other side. Then you trek back through the land of the dinosaurs. You manage to avoid any more rampaging giant lizards. At last you reach the point where the east and west routes meet up, on the other side of the great canyon dividing them.

 Turn to page 71.

You let out a gasp of terror. Attached to the six-inch fangs poking through the leaves is a saber-tooth tiger! And it's ready to pounce!

With lightning speed you leap into the pit to your left, avoiding the tiger's attack by inches. No sooner do you hit the bottom of the pit than your body is wrenched the other way. You find yourself going *up!*

"*Whoooaaa!*" you cry. Your leg is caught in a vine rope, which is attached to a high tree branch. You've jumped into a trap. Now you're dangling upside down above the pit!

The tiger paws at you like a cat reaching for a piece of string, but you swing just out of its reach. Suddenly a bloodcurdling yell comes from the forest. Ralph charges out of the trees with a spear poised over his shoulder. The tiger takes one look at him and scampers away.

Ralph looks at you and explodes with laughter. "Snaggletooth find new toy," he says, trying to catch his breath as you swing over the pit.

"Yeah, yeah, very funny. Now get me down from here!"

Ralph's expression abruptly turns stubborn. "Time

Blatt," he demands. "You help find Time Blatt, we go home."

You glare at him. He folds his arms.

Dangling upside down, with your blood rushing to your brain, you're forced to do some quick reasoning. You have to face the fact that somehow or other you've washed up on an island that is home to an incredible array of prehistoric animals.

You also can't deny that Ralph saved your life. He's pretty macho, even for a Neanderthal. It's a dog-eat-dog, cat-eat-kid world out there. He might be the key to your survival. And who knows, maybe there's something to his Time Blatt superstition.

"Okay, Ralph," you say. "We'll find the Time Blatt."

"Oof, oof! Oof, oof!" he exclaims, jumping up and down in some sort of Neanderthal celebration. Finally he cuts you down from the vine, chuckling again and mumbling, "Kitty toy."

You stand still for a moment to let the blood drain back into your body, where it belongs. Then you clap your hands and say, "Okay, Ralph, let's go look for that Time Blatt. But before we do, I want to build a signal fire in case my friends are out there. Help me gather some wood?"

With Ralph's help, you soon have a tall stack of kindling. You carry it to a bluff above the beach. After adding some dry moss as tinder, you take a match from a waterproof packet on your survival belt. You strike the match and set the moss afire.

Ralph stares at you with wide eyes. He backs away slowly, then bows down and says, "Great wizard, create fire. Rrrwwff bring meat offering." He runs off toward his cave.

"Maybe we'll be a good team after all, Ralph," you muse. "You take care of the wild animals and the food, and I'll do the wizardry."

He returns with two hunks of dripping red meat. You cook them over the fire. Meat on a stick hasn't tasted so good since they invented corn-dogs.

The sun starts to sink and you retreat to Ralph's cave for the night. He even gives you a buffalo skin to sleep on. "Tomorrow Time Blatt," he says happily, and starts to snore.

You move your buffalo skin to the other side of the cave. "Nothing personal, Ralph, but you sound like a bulldozer."

In the morning you set out on your search for the Time Blatt. Even if it doesn't exist, you don't mind doing some exploration. Now that you've gotten used to the idea of this crazy, mixed-up prehistoric island, you're starting to think it may be the most incredible scientific discovery ever made. If you ever make it back, that is . . .

Ralph first leads you up the slope of a small mountain. There are dead trees everywhere. Many trunks on the slope are blackened or charred by lightning. It's an ominous beginning for your journey. They stand like eerie skeletons and you wonder what tales they could tell if they could talk.

Suddenly you stop short. You think you see something carved into the blackened trunk of one of the trees. What does it say? You take a closer look. The tree has been hollowed out by fire. Should you reach inside the charred trunk?

If you reach inside the tree, turn to page 42.

If you stay away from it, turn to page 7.

You gently pick up the dinosaur egg. "What
happened, little fellow? You look like you fell
out of the nest."

You can hardly believe you're holding an actual dinosaur egg in your hand. You notice a slight crack along
one side. "You're about to be born, aren't you," you say.
"We need to get you to a safe, warm place."

As you search for a good home for the egg, you sense
that you're being followed. But when you turn around,
nothing is there .

Almost by accident, you come upon a nest in the crook
of a fallen tree. Five other eggs sit snugly in the nest.
Carefully you put the missing egg back in its place.

At that moment you hear clicking sounds from behind
you. You turn around. What you see nearly makes you
jump backward into the nest.

 Turn to page 50.

You approach the left half of the bizarre creature. And since that's the vicious reptile half, armored with spikes and spines and claws and plates, Ralph has his club poised to attack as he follows cautiously behind you.

The creature makes a kind of spitting, growling noise at you. "You are the strangest thing I've ever seen," you taunt it. "Now why don't you just let us go by?"

It hisses more loudly and flicks a long, snake-like tongue at you. Ralph picks up a big rock. You keep edging toward the beast.

"Run!" Ralph cries, and hurls the rock. It makes a direct hit on the creature's nose, but just bounces off its armored plates.

You've already taken two steps by then. The creature's head whips around and spews a long stream of vile green liquid at you. It hits you square in the face.

"I'm burning up!" you cry to Ralph, trying to wipe the liquid away from your eyes. But it's sticky. You just end up spreading it around.

It becomes harder and harder to move your limbs. You

sink to your knees, feeling very weak. You have been paralyzed by some very fast-acting nerve toxin. The creature watches you from a safe distance. Most likely you will be its next meal.

The last thing you see is Ralph fleeing back toward the water. You hope that somehow or other he'll be able to get past the horrid creature and find the Time Blatt. But for you, time has stopped—forever.

The End

Look here," you murmur, reading the words carved on the charred tree stump.

You reach inside. Your hand touches something cool and smooth. You pull it out. It's an old wine bottle with a note inside. You use a stick to extract the note. It's starting to crumble, but you can read most of it. "Thank goodness I'm taking Spanish in school. It's half in Spanish," you say as you scan the faded ink.

You explain the note to Ralph, who has never seen writing before. "It was written by a sixteenth-century Spanish conquistador. His ship was struck by lightning, and he ended up on this island. He says the island has many different regions, each with its own marvelous monsters. Apparently the regions are separated by gorges."

You scan the note and then read out loud, "'I alone have discovered an escape from this forsaken place and a way to return home. You must travel the ancient ground, in and out of millenia, to the beginning of time. Be stout and fearless, for many are the dangers on the way. There be many furnaces at the beginning of time. And in the eye of the tallest volcano will you find the fantastic *blato de tiempo*. I leave the rest up to you.' It is signed, Señor Fernando Rodrigo Veracruz the Intrepid."

You grab Ralph and shake him. "You were right! There really *is* a Time Blatt! But we have to go to the beginning of time to find it. Since the island is full of prehistoric animals, we'll always know what period we're in. We'll just keep going further back in the earth's history until we get to the beginning."

"Oof, oof," responds Ralph.

 Turn to page 25.

"Paddle hard!" you scream to Ralph. "There's a huge sea monster underneath us!"

You and Ralph push at the water with your arms and legs and struggle to bring the raft about. But you hardly get going before the thing underneath you rises. You're lifted into the air. You and Ralph cling desperately to the raft, but it tilts sideways on the scaly monster's back. You lose your grip and plunge into the water with a big splash.

This catches the eye of the beast. Now you can see what it is: a kronosaur, king of the primeval waters. It is over forty feet long. It has a massive dinosaurlike body, with a gaping ten-foot-wide jaw and the teeth of a shark.

It moves with the help of huge paddlelike flippers. You swim away from it as fast as you can. It's slow but big. In seconds, the shadow of its tremendous jaw falls over you. You can even see the outline of its terrible teeth cast on the water. It is the shadow of death.

The End

"Let's go west!" you announce. It's hard to resist the landscape of dinosaurs and giant Jurassic ferns. Is that an apatosaur you see in the distance? Getting an up-close look at the huge lizards is a scientist's dream. Besides, you're not sure if Ralph could build a raft strong enough to cross the vast lakes you saw to the east.

You and Ralph tromp down the other side of the mountain, heading west. A small gorge separates the mountain from the next landscape you enter: the Land of the Dinosaurs.

Here the air is thick and steamy. There are ferns as tall as trees, along with conifers, cycads, and ginkgos. You tread lightly and follow Ralph. All around you are amazing beasts: a gargantuan apatosaur, a long-necked diplodocus, a spine-backed stegosaur. You even see a pack of hungry allosaurs. You only get a glimpse, though, before Ralph grabs you and makes you hide in a tree until they go away.

Near the end of the day, you stop for a rest in a clearing surrounded by giant ferns and low conifers. All is quiet. "We're on the right track," you tell Ralph. "We're going back in time." But Ralph seems concerned. He kneels down and presses his ear to the ground.

Jumping up, he puts a hand on your arm. You listen, and then you hear it: a rumble, so low-pitched that you can barely pick it up. But you can feel the vibrations in the ground through your feet. Whatever is coming, it's huge and powerful. You look around you but all you see are trees.

It's getting louder now. The ground is shaking. You and Ralph circle around the clearing trying to locate the source of all the noise. The rumble is a roar in your ears. You want nothing more than to turn and run, except that you're afraid you could run right into whatever it is.

"There!" you cry as a shape appears out of the trees. "Ralph, what do we do?"

"*Oooooof!*" is all Ralph can say as he dashes for the trees to your left.

 If you follow Ralph, turn to page 54.

 If you dive the other way, turn to page 63.

Normally you wouldn't think of eating a dinosaur egg. But right now all you can think of is filling your tummy. So you'll cook the egg, peel it, and eat it. You can almost see a dino-sized omelette laid out before you with a little dash of salt and pepper.

You gather kindling and soon you have a nice blaze going. You're in the process of trying to figure out how to hold the egg out over the fire when you see them: two reptilian eyes staring at you from the bushes. Actually, they're not staring at *you*, they're staring at the egg. They belong to a five-foot tall oviraptor.

Your catalogue-like brain informs you that oviraptors are nest-raiders and love to eat eggs. "Oh, so you want my egg, do you?" you say. "Well, forget it. I found it, and I'm eating it."

With one hand you reach for the egg. The oviraptor cocks her head. She doesn't look hungry, but she's serious about something. That's funny, you think.

Just in time, you see the oviraptor springing for an attack. You jump away, hoping she doesn't follow. But she's not interested in you. For a moment you watch her nuzzle the egg but she doesn't eat it. Then it dawns on you. It's *her* egg! You slip back into the underbrush.

Eventually you do learn what seeds and plants you can eat in the prehistoric world. That's because you are eating them for the rest of your life. You never find Ralph or the Time Blatt. But you do find a lot of dinosaurs—and eventually one of them finds you . . . absolutely delicious.

The End

Standing right there is a small dinosaur. Well, small by dinosaur standards—she's only as tall as you are. You recognize her as an oviraptor, a pack hunter and a meat-eater. While you stare nervously at her deadly talons, she's peering around you at the nest.

You carefully step aside. The raptor runs up to the nest. Making more clicking sounds, she gently turns over each egg with her muzzle.

"You're the mom," you say slowly.

She cocks her head at you. "I wish somebody would take me back to *my* nest," you add. "Or at least back to my Ralph," you say nostalgically and add a little "oof, oof!"

The raptor suddenly cocks her head the other way. You repeat your *oof oof*. Then she makes some new clicking sounds. She runs a few feet away from the nest, stops, and looks at you. You don't know what to do. She takes a few more steps, stops, and waits.

"What, you want me to follow?" you ask. You move toward her. She runs a little farther and stops to wait.

Soon you are galloping through the ferns and palms behind a real-live oviraptor. You have no idea where she's
taking you, but you can tell that you've made another
prehistoric friend.

You are puffing hard trying to keep up with the speedy
raptor. Even when she takes you down into a gorge, you
follow her.

Suddenly she makes a sharp turn and vanishes. You
find yourself all alone in the bottom of a deep gorge.
"Hello?" you call. "Hello?"

You listen for an answer. Then you hear a plaintive
wail from farther up the gorge. You move toward it. It
becomes a kind of howl. Before you know it, you run
smack dab into something large and furry. At first you
try to escape, but then you inhale a familiar stench. You
are wrapped in Ralph's smelly embrace.

"Oof! Oof!" he grunts joyfully. Then he complains,
"Wizard run away! Rrrwwff eat meat without fire."

"Meat?" you demand. "Where?"

Ralph produces a slab from inside his animal skin.
You're so hungry you almost grab it. But starving as you
are, you still can't stomach raw meat. "I didn't run away,"
you tell Ralph as you quickly build yourself a fire. "I was
being chased by a crazed triceratops. Where did you go,
anyway? I looked all over for you."

Ralph looks a little sheepish. "Rrrwwff see meat. Hunt
meat. Kill meat. Eat meat."

"You're *such* a Neanderthal. Well, at least you saved a little for me." You thrust your meat onto a stick and cook it over the fire.

"It's lucky I made friends with that oviraptor and she knew where you were," you say when you're finished eating. You wash the meat down with some rainwater. "Do you have any idea where we are? Or which way we should go?"

Ralph shrugs twice. "Get out of hole. Look around."

Just then, a hoarse bellow comes from the top of the gorge. You look up. A giant shape is outlined against the sky. What is it? You know you need to get out of the gorge, but which way's the right way? Should you climb toward the shape? Or should you go back the way you came with the oviraptor?

 If you go back toward the dinosaurs, turn to page 32.

 If you climb out of the gorge on the side where the beast is, turn to page 74.

"**W**ait for me!" you yell and chase after Ralph, adrenaline pumping. You reach him in three quick powerful strides. But your legs get caught in his and you both go sprawling to the forest floor.

"*Aargh!*" he cries. But it's too late for that. The charging triceratops is already upon you. The last thing you see are the two razor-sharp horns on the top of his massive head—one for each of you.

The End

"Any port in a storm," you murmur, following Ralph toward the "island"—which you can see is actually a mammoth sea turtle, the size of a house. Ralph grasps the edge of the shell and lifts himself onto it. He gives you a hand up and you both scramble to the top.

Once you've had a chance to catch your breath, you turn to Ralph. "Let's hope it doesn't dive," you say.

Ralph pats the creature's shell. "Nice hide-a-head. No dive. No make Rrrwwff swim."

Suddenly the island is moving. You and Ralph hold on to each other. The giant turtle chugs along at a steady clip. Even better, it's going in the right direction—toward the beginning of time. But you're on the alert, prepared for it to dive at any moment.

But by the time your prehistoric ocean liner finally sinks into the water, you're close enough to shore that even Ralph can swim to land without much trouble.

You come dripping out of the water. But you can't go any farther. Blocking your way is a creature you've never seen in any of your dinosaur books—a creature so

56

bizarre, it could only have come from this crazy island. It's a creature with two heads. One end snarls at you, while the other gives you a curious look. Which way will you go? Which half do you think you should take on?

 If you approach the half on your left, turn to page 40.

 If you approach the half on your right, turn to page 62.

You pass by the funny-shaped object at your feet and plunge deeper into the cave. Desperately you search for the Time Blatt. You know you only have a few seconds to find it before the next eruption of scalding steam.

Unfortunately, the moment you go deeper into the cave, you lose the last bit of light filtering in from outside. You can only feel around blindly in the dark. You never see the scorching blast of steam that comes roaring up from the bowels of the earth. But you hear its roar. A moment later you feel it—as you are boiled like a cabbage in a pot.

The End

"Jump ship!" you cry to Ralph. Without hesitation, you plunge into the water.

"*Aaargh*," he objects, but he follows you.

You swim away from the raft as fast as you can. Ralph dog-paddles after you, splashing and spluttering. You turn to see the raft being lifted into the air on the back of a giant sea monster.

It's a massive kronosaur, the king of the seagoing reptiles. Attached to its forty-foot body is a ten-foot-long sharp-toothed jaw like a shark's. It emits a mighty roar as the raft slides off its back.

The gargantuan reptile doesn't seem to notice you and Ralph as you slip away. Instead, it fixes its beady eye on the raft. In a single strike it chomps your raft in two. The raft timbers splinter like toothpicks in its monstrous mouth. You just keep swimming.

Only after the immense beast has returned to the deep do you realize the trouble you're in. You're a pretty good swimmer, but Ralph is panting hard. You point to a shoreline a ways off to your right and ask Ralph, "Can you make it?"

Ralph gestures at what appears to be a small island immediately to your left. You hadn't noticed it before. "No, there!" he pants.

You start to swim with him, trying to get a closer look at the island. What kind of island is it?

 If you swim toward the small island, turn to page 55.

 If you tell Ralph not to go that way, turn to page 70.

"Y̲ou are one mixed-up beast," you say as you approach the right half of the bizarre creature blocking your way. It seems to be half bird, half reptile—and each half has its own head. The half on your left is a nasty affair of spines, armor, and long sharp teeth. But the half on your right is soft and curious and wide-eyed.

"I found you. I get to name you. I think I'll dub you *Mixedosaurus schizophrenicus*," you say, drawing closer to the creature on the right. It makes a kind of whining, cooing sound.

Ralph follows behind. He's dug up a handful of sea worms in the soft mud near the water. He offers one to the creature, which nibbles at it, then gulps them all down.

You and Ralph slip past the creature while it gobbles up the rest of the worms. As you walk along, you discover you've reached the end of your sea journey. You are on the other side of the great canyon that divided the east and west routes. The Time Blatt can't be far.

 Turn to page 71.

It's seven tons of charging triceratops! You can see almost nothing but the twin horns above its nose.

You don't have time to worry about Ralph. You dive out of the way. Ralph dives the other way. The triceratops charges right between the two of you.

You get to your feet, brush yourself off, and start to heave a sigh of relief. But then you hear Ralph cry, "Oof! Look out! Noseforks turns around!"

He's charging you again! You flee into the tree ferns at the edge of the clearing. You can hear the giant horned beast tromping after you, splintering trees and mashing shrubs. You plunge blindly through the underbrush. Some instinctive part of your brain has taken over. You're thinking only of survival.

Finally you collapse at the base of a tall cedar. In between panting breaths, you listen for sounds of the rampaging dinosaur. The ground no longer shakes. There's no low rumbling sound in the distance. It seems you've escaped him.

But where are you? You sit up. You don't even remember which direction you came from in your panic. You were just running any which way you could to save your life.

"Ralph?" you call out timidly. You hear nothing. You call again a little louder this time. Pretty soon you're yelling as loudly as you can. "Ralph! Where in the world are you?"

You wander around for a little while until finally you slump down in frustration. Darkness is falling. You make a little bed of ferns and lie down for the night, feeling more lost and alone than you ever have in your life.

You wake up feeling starved. Ralph never had a chance to hunt down any food yesterday, so you haven't eaten since the day before. The first thing you do, after a stretch and a yawn, is set off in search of something to eat.

But all of the plants are so unfamiliar to you. You try to remember if fruits and berries had come into existence yet during the Jurassic.

Then you stumble across something sitting right in the middle of your path. You're so hungry, it looks delicious. But should you eat it? You stop and think.

Should you build a fire and roast it? Or take it to a safer place?

 If you want to eat it, turn to page 48.

 If you take it to a safe place, turn to page 38.

"Let's go east," you say to Ralph after looking at the watery landscape. "Fewer monsters that way. You're sure you can build a raft that will take us across those lakes?"

"No problem," Ralph says with a wave of his hand.

"There are too many dinosaurs on the other side. I'd hate for our adventure to be ended by an angry allosaur," you add with a shiver.

Ralph shakes his head vigorously and shivers too. He starts down the east side of the mountain, and you follow. When you arrive at the shore, you discover the water is actually salt water, and the "lakes" are really a series of shallow seas.

You and Ralph set to work building a raft from fallen timbers. You lash it together with strong vines. Ralph fashions a sail from some very large, tough prehistoric leaves.

You're a little nervous when you put the raft into the water. But once you've been out for a while, you begin to relax. A soft breeze pushes you across the gentle waves. The raft seems sturdy enough.

You pass a pleasant day sailing Mesozoic seas. Sometimes you are out on open water, sometimes passing through swamps. You witness an astonishing variety of prehistoric life. Pteranodons, with their anvil-shaped heads, soar through the sky above you. When you pass near land, you occasionally glimpse early mammals scuttling about in the foliage, trying to avoid the giant lizards.

As the day goes on, you see creatures from still earlier times. An archaeopteryx, one of the earliest birds, uses its teeth to chew up insects and lizards on land while a plesiosaur, a long-necked paddler, chases schools of fish beneath you.

"This is indeed a pleasant way to spend a day," you declare to Ralph. He grunts "oof oof" in reply.

"It's also good that we're seeing animals from earlier periods," you go on. "It means we're getting closer to the beginning, where the Time Blatt is."

But Ralph suddenly seems preoccupied by something in the water. You follow his eye and notice some unusual ripples. Then you feel a kind of trembling. Your boat feels unsteady.

You look at Ralph. His eyes are open wide in alarm. If he's scared, you know you should be, too! But where is the motion coming from? You scan the murky water around you. Nothing appears on the surface.

Then you feel a gentle rocking motion under the raft. Something makes you look down between the timbers of the raft. You let out a scream. What is it?

 If you jump ship into the murky water, turn to page 59.

 If you tell Ralph to help you paddle the raft away, turn to page 44.

"**R**alph, come back!" you call. "That's not an island! It's a giant sea turtle!"

Ralph ignores you. But you refuse to follow him. You've just had one run-in with a monster of the sea. You're not about to take on an overgrown amphibian.

"I'll meet you on the shore," you call to Ralph. You can't tell if he hears.

You turn your energies to swimming for the far shore. But it is much farther away than you expect. You swim and swim and swim, but the shore is still impossibly far away.

At some point you realize you're not going to make it. You have no reserves of energy left. It is a relief when you finally stop swimming and give rest to your weary bones.

As you sink into the deep, your last thought is to wonder whether one day your fossils will be discovered. And if they are, you wonder what scientists will make of them, down at the bottom of the prehistoric sea.

The End

On the horizon ahead you can see plumes of smoke floating above a series of volcanoes.

"There's Señor Rodrigo's furnace at the beginning of time," you tell Ralph. "We're getting close to the Time Blatt. We just have to find the tallest volcano—and somehow get into its eye."

Ralph makes a face. "What if volcano eats us?"

"Let's hope it spits us out." You set out through a new landscape, the stark terrain of the Paleozoic Era. You see sailback reptiles such as the dimetredon, and the very strange anteosaur, a hairy reptile that looks something like a lion. Dragonflies with thirty-inch wingspans buzz through the air, while on the ground you must dodge scorpions and armored millipedes as long as you are tall! Although he doesn't want to admit it, you can tell Ralph is little bit freaked out by these colossal bugs. You've seen them before in science books, and you know that as long as you stay out of their way, you'll be okay.

The landscape changes yet again. Mosses and horsetails take the place of trees and ferns. Only smaller, insectlike animals remain.

Finally all signs of life die out. The land is bare rock.

You *must* be near the beginning of life on earth.

You arrive at the edge of a precipice. Across the way, plumes of smoke fill the sky.

"There it is!" cries Ralph.

You peer through the billowing fumes. Do you see what Ralph sees?

 Turn to page 12.

At least the megatherium at the top of the gorge is some sign of life. You know the giant sloth is a plant-eater, so it's not going to eat *you*. You point Ralph that way.

"Meat!" proclaims Ralph.

"No, Ralph, leave it alone. It's way too big for us to kill."

Ralph grumbles. "Why go toward slobberbeast?" He pounds his chest. "Rrrwwff live with slobberbeast. Hunt. Run away from. Whatever."

You stop in your tracks. "You're right, Ralph. I wasn't thinking. The megatherium is a mammal. It's from a much later stage of evolution, the Pleistocene period, which is back where we started. Señor Rodrigo said we have to go back to the beginning of time to find the Time Blatt—which means going back toward the dinosaurs."

Ralph gives a sharp nod of approval. He's pretty smart for a caveman. You turn around and trek back through the land of the dinosaurs until you reach the point where the east and west routes meet up.

 Turn to page 71.

I t's an alarm clock! You can hardly believe your eyes. You pick it up and stumble out of the cave just as a new burst of smoke comes pouring up from the depths of the mountain. Coughing, you cry, "I've got it!"

Ralph is jumping up and down. "Great Wizard find Time Blatt! Oof oof!"

"The only question is, how does it work?" You shake it but you don't hear a single 'tick.'

Ralph grabs it from you, sets it on a rock, and falls to his knees. Bowing to the object, he chants, "Mighty Time Blatt, take us home!"

You watch him. What the heck, you think, maybe it'll work. You get on your knees with Ralph and bow down to the alarm clock, repeating Ralph's words.

Nothing happens. The rumbling under the mountain increases. Thunder booms from the clouds. Electricity crackles all around you. It's time to move.

You pick up the Time Blatt and pop open a little compartment on the back. You see that it's empty except for the line of fine print on the cover: Batteries not included.

"I can't believe this!" you say, spluttering. "Do you mean to tell me we can't go back home just because I didn't remember to bring a stupid pair of batteries?"

"Batteries?" Ralph asks.

"Yeah, you know—electricity." You gesture at the crackling sky above. "That's how these things work."

"Huh?" says Ralph.

Suddenly a great roar begins beneath you. It rises in power until you feel as if the whole world is coming apart.

"The volcano is erupting!" you cry.

Molten lava is rising from the bowels of the earth and pouring out of the mouth of the volcano. Black ash spews from the mountain and rains down all around you. It feels as if the earth is about to come to an end—even though you know it's just beginning!

"Do something, great wizard!" Ralph demands.

A huge black cloud now hovers above you. Suddenly something flashes out of it! What should you do?

 If you take cover, turn to page 78.

 If you hold up the Time Blatt, turn to page 82.

"Look out!" you cry to Ralph as lightning crackles and streaks across the sky.

Ralph lets out a scream of terror. You both try to duck out of the way. But there is no place to take cover. If you go into the cave, you'll be boiled by gusts of steam. Instead, you cower by the side of a boulder.

It offers little protection. The huge force of electricity gathering in the cloud above you lets loose. A lightning bolt of incredible power streaks to the ground. Nothing is left of you and Ralph but a few charred teeth.

The End

"Come on, Ralph!" you say, grabbing his arm and pulling him toward the giant quetzalcoatlus that has landed nearby. "This is probably our only chance." You each jump on one of its wings, which span fifty feet from tip to tip.

The gigantic flying reptile takes a couple of steps, then drops off the edge of the precipice. Its mighty wings begin to beat, and it lifts into the air. You and Ralph hold on for dear life.

The quetzalcoatlus transports you across the churning, flaming waters of the primordial gorge. As you approach the volcano, you notice two deep caves right across from each other, set into the side of the mountain.

The great winged reptile touches down a little ways below the crater at the top of the volcano. You and Ralph scramble off. "Thanks for the ride," you call out as it disappears back into the billowing clouds of smoke.

A constant rumble comes from inside the mountain. The air is thick with ash and smoke and fumes. The smell of sulfur nearly makes you gag. Ralph gazes fearfully at the belching mouth of the volcano. "Rrrwwff wait here. Wizard find Time Blatt."

"I don't think we have to go up there, Ralph," you answer. "Rodrigo said the *eye* of the volcano, not the mouth. When we flew in, I saw two caves in the mountain that looked like eyes. They're right below us."

You make your way down the mountain to the caves below. All the while, the sky overhead seems to be on fire. A light rain begins to fall from the clouds. The water stings your skin like acid.

A stream of hot smoke and sulfurous fumes is rushing out of the cave. The eruption stops, then repeats half a minute later. "It seems to blow every twenty-five seconds, like a geyser," you say. "I'm going in after the next one."

You time your moment, then rush in. You nearly trip on an object lying in the middle of the cave. What is it that you see? Should you pick it up and get out of there? Or go farther into the cave to look for the Time Blatt?

 If you pick up the object, turn to page 75.

 If you go farther into the cave, turn to page 58.

Y ou hold the Time Blatt up to the lightning streaking across the sky. It comes to you in a flash: A bolt of lightning is what brought you, Ralph, and Señor Rodrigo all to this island. It must be the energy source that activates the Time Blatt.

The massive voltage of electrical energy accumulating in the cloud above you lets loose in a tremendous bolt of lightning. It streaks directly to the Time Blatt and it starts to ring like crazy. Your arms shake as if they're about to come off. Your hair stands straight up on end. Then you black out.

When you open your eyes again, you're floating on your back in the deep blue water of the Caribbean. The sky is clear, except for a few puffy clouds in the distance. Voices are calling from behind you.

You turn around. It's the *Trilobite!*

You swim toward the ship. It comes about, and soon you see Ernesto at the stern. As he tosses you another lifeline, he laughs in relief. "We thought you were eaten up by the Bermuda Triangle!" he exclaims as he pulls you back on board.

"I was," you say quietly.

Soon Bill and the others are there to welcome you back aboard. "What happened to your scuba tanks?" Bill asks.

"Must have lost them in the storm," you answer.

"That storm was something else," Bill agrees. "Here one minute, gone the next. Strangest thing I've ever seen."

One of the scientists hums the *Twilight Zone* theme. Then and there you decide that, except for Ernesto, no one else will ever know of your voyage to Prehistoric Island.

Late at night, gazing out at the stars in the black sky, you do tell Ernesto your story. But you know that if you said a word about it to the scientists, they'd think you swallowed a little too much salt water and pickled your brain.

Instead, over the course of the summer's work, you gradually show off the knowledge you gained on the island. The scientists are dazzled by your insights. They keep asking you how you know so much about the prehistoric world. You just smile and say, "I guess you just had to be there." They can only give you puzzled looks.

Your sole regret is that you never got to say good-bye to Ralph. You figure he must have gotten back to Neanderthal-land at the same time you found the *Trilobite*. He's the only one who really understands what you went through. You wonder what he told *his* friends when he got home.

The End

SOLUTIONS

p.vii: Allosaurus

p.5: Giant shrimp

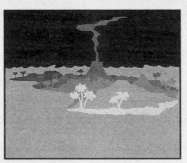

p.11: Island

p.13: Quetzalcoatlus

p.15: Caveman

SOLUTIONS

p.21: Saber-tooth tiger

p.23: Jurassic landscape

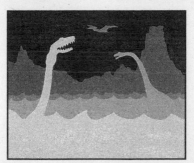

p.27: Water landscape

p.31: Mastodon

p.37: Look Here

SOLUTIONS

p.39: Oviraptor

p.47: Triceratops

p.53: Megatherium

p.57: Beast with two heads

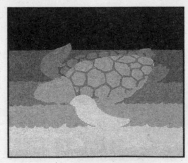

p.61: Giant sea turtle

SOLUTIONS

p.65: Egg

p.69: Kronosaur

p.73: Volcano

p.77: Lightning

p.81: Alarm clock

ABOUT THE CONTRIBUTORS

JAY LEIBOLD grew up in Denver, Colorado and now lives in San Francisco, California. He has written fourteen interactive books for the Choose Your Own Adventure series, which is also published by Bantam Books, and six books in the *Dojo Rats* series for young adults. He is the author of *Treasure Hunt*, the first book in the Super Eye Adventure series.

RAY "3-D" ZONE is the king of 3-D comics. Over a ten-year period he has produced or published one hundred 3-D comics featuring such characters as Batman, Flash Gordon, The Rocketeer, Krazy Kat and Rat Fink. In addition to comic book scripting, he has written numerous articles about popular culture for a variety of publications.

CHUCK ROBLIN was born in Hollywood, California in 1949. Roblin is the creator of *Tex Benson*, a Cold War aviation story taking place in the distant future, which ran as a syndicated daily and Sunday strip in European newspapers for over a decade. It was published as a comic book in the states in 3-D by The 3-D Zone and now is called *Zori Stories*.